Collins

FOOTBALL FANATIC

BOGGIES

cake

Steve Barlow & Steve Skidmore

Chapter 1

Unbelievable news! I just watched the draw for the FA Cup Third Round. My team, Mudchester FC (nickname, the Boggies) have been drawn at home against Kingston FC!

Kingston won the Premier League last year. Their team is stuffed full of famous players from all over the world. This will be the biggest game ever in the Boggies' history.

FA Cup Third Round Draw: **Mudchester FC - Kingston FC**

My mate Dave Langley (everyone calls him Dangley) says the Boggies have got no chance. He is a traitor! He was born in Mudchester, so he should be a Boggies fan like me.

But he says he only wants to support a good team, so he reckons he's a Kingston fan. Yeah, right – he lives over 200 miles from London and he's never been to their ground!

You just wait! When the Boggies beat Kingston, I'm going to chant the score to Dangley every minute of every day until his brain explodes.

The trouble is, we've only won a few games this season, and we only won one of those because the other team didn't turn up.

It's not easy supporting the bottom team in the football league … We are below everyone!

POS	TEAM	PLD	WON	DRN	LOST	PTS
21	ASHTON ATHLETIC	23	7	6	10	27
22	UPFIELD WANDERERS	23	6	7	10	25
23	RENTON ROVERS	22	6	5	11	23
24	MUDCHESTER FC	22	6	4	12	22

●●● SPORT

Chapter 2

I went to see the Boggies playing Renton Rovers yesterday. They're one place above us in the table, so it should have been a close match, but it wasn't. We lost 4–1.

We should never have lost, as we had most of the play and Kevin "Wrong-Way" Tibbs hit the post three times.

Unfortunately it was our post.

The Rovers fans chanted, "Should have gone to Specsavers".

Harsh, but fair.

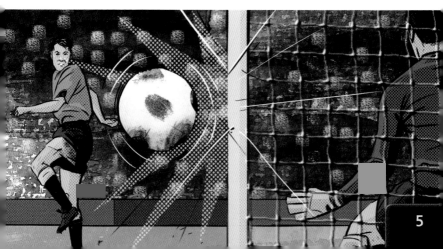

Our star striker, Dermot Doodie, played like a camel with four left feet. I drew a picture of him.

I couldn't believe it! He's usually our best player. He wants to get a transfer to a bigger club, but I hope he doesn't, as he's my favourite player.

And the ref should never have sent Tim "Mad Dog" Terry off.

It was a fifty-fifty ball, so it was a harsh decision. Although the player Terry smacked did get sent to hospital in two separate ambulances.

OUCH!

The day after the Renton game I got an email from Dangley.

From: "dave langley" <dave.langley@mainline.net>

To: Alex Roberts <boggiesfan@AWOL.com>

Date: Thurs, Dec 8th, 08:30

Subject: Boggies lose (again)

I see your rubbish team lost again last night. My sister says her Brownies pack will give Mudchester a game. She says they promise to go easy, to give you a chance. I reckon the Brownies would still win.

In fact, your team shouldn't be called the Boggies, they should be called the Bogeys – because they're **snot** very good.

Dave

Not funny.

Chapter 3

I got my ticket for the Big Match today.

It made me feel like the game is really going to happen! The mighty Kingston are really coming here, to Bogside Park, Mudchester!

I hope they've got a good map.

In fact, being a season ticket holder for the Boggies, I got two tickets. All my mates at school (who only turn up at Boggies matches when they feel like it) are dead jealous. Dangley has been asking me to let him have my spare ticket. He can get lost. He's not having it after sending me that email. Even if he begs me.

Chapter 4

It's Christmas! What's more important, it's only two weeks to go before the Kingston game!

I can't believe how much Boggies stuff I got for Christmas. I mentioned to *one or two* people that I'd like something to take to the match, but I didn't expect *everyone* to buy me Boggies gear and *nothing else.*

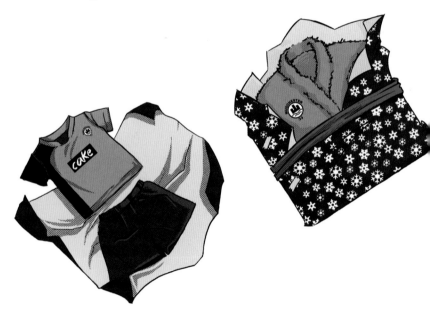

I pulled the presents from under the tree and opened them up.

I got: home kit, away kit, pre-match kit, scarf, beanie hat, touchline jacket, gloves, dressing gown, slippers, pen set, mug, keyring, watch, soap, bath towel, bedspread, air freshener (I reckon that came from Dangley …), rubber duck, shirt-over-the-head gnome…

Never mind – Boxing Day tomorrow. The Boggies are playing Seaport Town in the league, and we really need the points!

Chapter 5

Great game against Seaport today! The Boggies were brilliant!

I felt a bit of an idiot walking to the ground. Mum made me wear all the different kit I got for Christmas (luckily, not the dressing gown and slippers).

I wore so many layers that people were pointing at me, laughing and yelling rude remarks.

But when the match started, I forgot all that. Seaport are a good side, but our lads were better.

Dermot Doodie scored twice and set up the third. It went in off "Wrong Way" Tibbs's backside, but who cares? Like our manager says, "They all count!"

We won 3–2. Another win could take us out of the drop zone for the first time this season.

RESULT! If we play like that against Kingston, we'll murder them!

Chapter 6

Then it got even better. I saw Dave Langley leaving the ground. He was actually wearing a Mudchester scarf.

"What are you doing here?" I asked him.

"I've been thinking about what you said," he replied. "That you should support your local team, so I thought I'd come along."

I couldn't believe I'd heard him say that. Dangley supporting the Boggies? Amazing!

"Did you enjoy the match?" I said.

He nodded. "Doodie played well."

"Yes, he did," I said.

"The Boggies did all right, didn't they?" he continued. "I reckon I should be following them."

How awesome was that!

If we're starting to win games for a change and even Dangley's taking an interest, I reckon the Boggies have got a chance against Kingston.

Maybe I'll let Dangley have my spare ticket after all ...

I wanted to remember the team that beat Seaport, so I kept the team pic from the programme:

ROW:

lad "The Impaler" Blaga, John "Leave it" Lewis,
oss "Blinky" Sanders (Goalkeeper), Tim "Mad Dog" Terry,
om "Lefty" Johnson, Nelson Basoli

NT ROW:

ed "Wheezy" Wright, Andy "Apeman" Armstrong, Dermot Doodie,
evin "Wrong Way" Tibbs, Esso Besso, Will Crosby (Manager·)

Chapter 7

It's finally here! The BIG MATCH DAY!

I woke up at 6:30 and got dressed in my Boggies kit.

It was too early to go to the ground, so I had nothing to do but watch cartoons on the TV. I felt as if someone had been tying knots in my stomach.

Dangley came round, and we caught the bus together to Bogside Park.

We went in and took our seats. The Boggies' ground is really small, but there were already loads of people about.

Kingston had brought lots of fans. They chanted, "Who are you? Who are you?"

So we chanted, "We are the Boggies, Football is our game! We play at the Bogside, Mudchester is our name!"

The teams came out and we began chanting, "Boggies, Boggies!"

The atmosphere was incredible. I had butterflies in my stomach. Even Dangley looked excited.

"Let's hope we win," I said.

"Oh, I'm sure WE will," Dangley replied and gave me a strange grin. "No problem."

The teams lined up, the ref blew his whistle, and the match started!

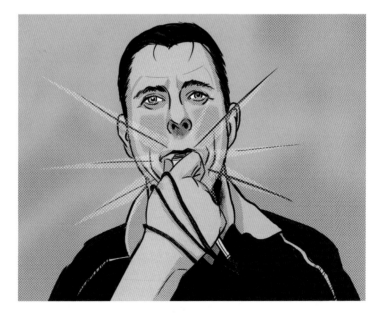

Chapter 8

For the first ten minutes, it was all Kingston.

They strolled through our defence. They got three corners and hit the post from one of them. The butterflies in my stomach had now turned into flying elephants.

Dangley looked as if he had ants in his pants. I thought he was just excited by the game, but it wasn't that.

As Kingston attacked again, he tore off his Boggies scarf. "What are you doing?" I screamed at him.

He pulled a Kingston scarf from his pocket and started waving it about and yelling, "King-ston! King-ston!"

THE TRAITOR!

Some of our supporters saw what he was doing. They didn't like that, so they tried to make him swallow the scarf.

The stewards had to rescue Dangley. Last time I saw him, the St John's Ambulance people were trying to pull the scarf out while he turned blue …

I was gutted. Dangley had tricked me! What an idiot I was.

Then it got even worse.

Kingston scored just before half-time. The Boggies had spent the whole first half hanging on, but everyone knew a Kingston goal was coming.

Kingston's number nine side-stepped a "Mad Dog" Terry tackle, left Blaga for dead and side-footed it into the net.

The ref blew for half-time. 1–0 down. Things were looking bad.

Chapter 9

I spent half-time just hoping that we wouldn't get too badly beaten.

But when the second half began, something incredible happened.

From the kick-off, Dermot Doodie made a run upfield. "Wrong Way" Tibbs, just for once, passed him an inch-perfect ball. Doodie ran on to it and …

GOAL! One all!

Every Boggies fan went crazy! We were screaming and jumping up and down and punching the air! What a feeling!

Kingston came back at us, but every time they shot at our goal, we just managed to keep it out of the net.

I was screaming and shouting along with all the Boggies fans.

Could we hold out against the mighty Kingston?

I yelled myself hoarse and bit my nails.

Then, in the last minute, Dermot Doodie got the ball again.

He wrong-footed the Kingston defence ...

He shot for goal …

… the ref blew for full time …

… the ball went into the net.

The crowd went mad! We'd WON!

But the ref waved his arms. He disallowed the goal! The ball had been in the air when he blew for full time. We'd drawn the game, not won it!

The crowd went mad again – but at the ref, this time.

I left the ground feeling very let down, like a balloon that's gone all wrinkly.

We'd nearly beaten the Champions, but we hadn't, and now there'd have to be a replay.

I didn't see Dangley. Lucky for him. He used me. I'm never going to speak to him again.

Ever.

Chapter 10

I tried to skive off school to queue for a replay ticket. But my mum told me if I did, she'd give my ticket to someone who deserved it.

Call that fair? I've supported the Boggies for years! If *I* don't deserve a ticket, who does?

By the time I got to the ground after school, there weren't any tickets left.

I was GUTTED!

Next day I met Dangley in the lunch queue. I hadn't seen him since he had to leave the match quickly.

He said, "All right, Alex?"

I said, "I'm not talking to you, you traitor!"

"That's a shame," he said. "I've got something you might be interested in."

"What's that, then?" I said.

"My dad's got me replay tickets for the Kingston match – and I've also got a spare."

Oh.

Dangley gave me a grin. "My dad says I can decide where it goes. Of course, if you're not *interested …"*

So there it was. I had to be nice to Dangley, and forgive him for being a traitor, or I wouldn't get to see the replay. But how can I be nice to someone like this …

Sometimes, life sucks. But then it got a whole lot worse.

"OK," I said. "I'll take the ticket and watch Doodie score the winner against you."

Dangley laughed. "Haven't you heard about him?"

I shook my head.

"Kingston have put in an offer to buy him. It's been accepted!"

My mouth dropped open. Our best player leaving? "But he won't be able to play for you against us," I said. "He's cup tied."

"Yeah, but it'll stop him playing for YOU!"

DOUBLE GUTTED!

Chapter 11

The papers are full of the news about Doodie's transfer. People are saying that you can't blame him.

Yes, I can! He's a bigger traitor than Dangley.

Without him playing against Kingston, we've got as much chance as a snowball in a heatwave.

I've taken down all my posters of him and burnt them. I've also peeled off his name from my Boggies shirt.

Who needs him?

Meanwhile, Dangley has been gloating about Doodie, and I can't say a thing.

Not only is he giving me the ticket, but his dad is going to drive me down to Kingston after school.

I wanted to go on the Boggies supporters' coach, but it leaves at midday. Once again, Mum wouldn't let me miss school.

What is it with her? Doesn't she realise what's important in life?

Chapter 12

On the day of the replay, Dangley's dad picked us up in his car, and we headed for the match.

Of course, Dangley made sure that the car was covered with Kingston scarves and flags.

And to make it worse, he started singing. "We've got the best team, in the land!"

I just sat staring glumly out of the window.

But then something brilliant happened …

Dangley's dad told him to shut up as he wanted to listen to Sports Chat on the radio.

He switched it on, and I couldn't believe what I was hearing.

The big news was that Doodie's transfer had fallen through! He hadn't passed a medical. He was going to be playing for the Boggies in the replay!

"YESSSSS!" I yelled. "GET IN!"

Dangley just stared out of the window.

We finally arrived at the Kingston stadium, and Dangley handed me a Kingston scarf.

"Put it on," he said.

"No way!" I replied. I knew I'd be sitting with the Kingston fans, but I wasn't going to wear a Kingston scarf.

Dangley shrugged. "Then you don't come in. You're not wearing your Mudchester scarf. You'd get thumped. So would I, for bringing you."

I put the scarf on, and we went in.

Chapter 13

I didn't really take in much of the pre-match build-up. The Kingston fans all around me were chanting and singing, but I was too busy trying not to be sick with nerves.

At least Doodie was playing. We had a chance!

The match started off quietly. Kingston passed the ball around easily. The Boggies seemed to be put off by playing in such a massive stadium.

The Boggies held their own for the first forty minutes. Then the trouble started.

"Mad Dog" Terry hardly touched Kingston's striker Leonardo, but all the blokes round me jumped up and yelled "Foul!"

Leonardo went down as if he'd been shot, rolling around and screaming in agony until the ref gave him a penalty just to shut him up!

Never mind, I thought, maybe "Blinky" Sanders will save it …

He didn't.

1–0 to Kingston. All the fans around me were going nuts, especially Dangley and his dad.

I still wasn't worried.

It was nearly half-time – there was only one goal in it and the whole second half to go.

We had Doodie playing for us, and he had something to prove to Kingston!

There was still everything to play for.

Chapter 14

How wrong can you be? The second half was a nightmare. The ref sent "Mad Dog" Terry off for a second yellow card. That was so wrong – Terry hardly *touched* Leonardo. Head wounds always bleed a lot. Everyone knows that.

After a few dabs of the magic sponge, Leonardo was okay again (surprise, surprise!). He led the next attack, and a minute or two later, he scored.

That was Game Over for the Boggies. Without "Mad Dog", they went to pieces, and Doodie didn't get a look in.

When the third goal went in, I just couldn't stop myself – I tore off my jacket and the Kingston scarf. I got my Mudchester scarf out of my pocket and held it up. "Boggies! Boggies!"

"Put it away," howled Dangley. "You'll get pulped!"

I didn't care. "Boggies! Boggies!"

Then something weird happened.

Some of the fans around me started laughing. One yelled, "Let's help him out, lads!"

And suddenly, all the fans around me were singing, "Boggies! Boggies!"

Of course, they were only doing it because they knew they were going to win. But they were showing some respect, too.

By the end of the game, all the Kingston fans around me were cheering for Mudchester.

We still lost, though.

Chapter 15

Next day, I downloaded a report about the match.

It didn't make easy reading.

BOGGIES BLITZED!

Kingston FC 8   0 Mudchester FC

Plucky Mudchester FC were torn apart by Kingston FC in a second half display of total football.

Mudchester held their own for much of the first half, but after the interval the London giants stepped up a gear to sink the Boggies

That was enough. I pressed delete.

So much for the "Romance of the Cup".
We were thrashed.

Back at school, Dangley asked me if I wanted to support Kingston now.

"No way!" I replied. I'm not one of these people who support clubs just because they're successful …

As they say, "Once a Boggie, always a Boggie!"

And of course, there's always next season … or the one after that … or the one after that … or the …

Reader challenge

Word hunt

 On page 25, find an adjective that describes a "croaky" voice.

 On page 34, find an adverb that means "unhappily".

 On page 41, find a verb that means "cried like a dog".

Story sense

 Why does Alex call his mate Dave Langley a traitor? (page 3)

 Why do you think Alex got so much Boggies gear for Christmas? (pages 10–11)

 Why was it such a surprise when Mudchester first scored against Kingston? (page 25)

Why was Alex not happy when he had to go to the match in Dave's dad's car? (pages 33–34)

Why do you think Alex wasn't worried when Mudchester were 1–0 down at half-time in the last match? (page 39)

Your views

9 Who did you think was going to win each
of the two matches between Kingston and
Mudchester? Give reasons.

10 Did you enjoy the story? Give reasons.

Spell it

With a partner, look at these words and then cover
them up.

- league
- screaming
- leave

Take turns for one of you to read the words aloud.
The other person has to try and spell each word.
Check your answers, then swap over.

Try it

With a partner, imagine you are doing a short TV
commentary for the final match in the story. Look
back at pages 38–43 and commentate on part of
the game that ended 8–0 to Kingston.

William Collins's dream of knowledge for all began with the publication of his first book in 1819. A self-educated mill worker, he not only enriched millions of lives, but also founded a flourishing publishing house. Today, staying true to this spirit, Collins books are packed with inspiration, innovation and practical expertise. They place you at the centre of a world of possibility and give you exactly what you need to explore it.

Collins. Freedom to teach.

Published by Collins Education
An imprint of HarperCollins*Publishers*
77–85 Fulham Palace Road
Hammersmith
London
W6 8JB

Browse the complete Collins Education catalogue at **www.collins.co.uk**

Series consultants: Alan Gibbons and Natalie Packer

10 9 8 7 6 5 4 3 2 1
ISBN 978-0-00-746474-6

British Library Cataloguing in Publication Data.
A catalogue record for this publication is available from the British Library.

Commissioned by Catherine Martin
Edited by Sue Chapple
Project-managed by Lucy Hobbs and Caroline Green
Illustration management by Tim Satterthwaite
Proofread by Hugh Hillyard-Parker
Typeset by Jouve India, Ltd
Production by Rebecca Evans
Printed and bound in China by South China Printing Co.
Cover design by Paul Manning

Acknowledgements

The publishers would like to thank the students and teachers of the following schools for their help in trialling the *Read On* series:

Park View Academy, London
Queensbury School, Bradford
Southfields Academy, London
St Mary's College, Hull
Ormiston Six Villages Academy, Chichester